101
Questions and
Answers about
Dangerous Animals

101

Questions
and
Answers
about
Dangerous
Animals

Seymour Simon

Illustrations by *E. Friedman*

Macmillan Publishing Company

New York

Collier Macmillan Publishers

London

Library of Congress Cataloging in Publication Data
Simon, Seymour.
101 questions and answers about dangerous animals.

Summary: Provides answers to 101 questions about the
habits and behavior of a variety of wild animals considered to be dangerous and describes the most dangerous
animal of all.
Includes index.
1. Dangerous animals—Miscellanea—Juvenile literature.
[1. Dangerous animals—Miscellanea.   2. Animals—Miscellanea.   3. Questions and answers]   I. Title.   II. Title:
One hundred one questions and answers about dangerous
animals.   III. Title: One hundred and one questions and
answers about dangerous animals.
QL100.S57 1985   591.6′5   84-42975
ISBN 0-02-782710-0

Contents

(1)

Mammals–
The Dangerous Cats

1. Which wild cats are the most dangerous?

The tiger, lion, leopard, and jaguar are probably the most dangerous of the cats. Nowadays, these four kinds of cats cause probably fewer than two dozen deaths each year. Most of the wild cats will avoid people whenever possible. But there always seem to be a few individuals that hunt people regularly.

The wild cats are excellent hunters. They are very powerful animals with great speed. The African lion charges its prey at forty miles per hour. The cheetah can speed over sixty miles per hour over level ground. The cats are also great leapers. The American puma is able to jump to the ground from a height of sixty feet.

All of the cats are able to swim, and many can climb trees. They have sharp senses, can learn quickly, and are usually hard to spot in their native surroundings. Many of the cats hunt at night, which makes it dangerous for people to travel after dark. In fact, the surprising thing about the big cats is that so few of them become human eaters.

2. How big are the dangerous cats?

The largest of the dangerous cats is the tiger. The now very rare Siberian tiger can reach a length of over ten feet from its nose to the tip of its tail and weigh over six hundred pounds. The Indian tigers are nearly as large, averaging about nine feet long and weighing about four hundred pounds. The African lion is about the same size as the Indian tiger.

The jaguar is the third largest of the dangerous cats, averaging about two hundred fifty pounds. The puma, leopard, and cheetah round out the order of size among the cats.

3. Which cat kills the most people?

Tigers probably kill more people each year than any other cat. Tigers are very strong. They grab their prey with their claws and clutch it within reach of their powerful jaws. Tigers can swim very well and can climb, though not as well as leopards. The tiger's eyesight is not very good, so tigers depend upon their hearing and sense of smell when hunting. The tiger eats an enormous amount of food and will stay with its dead prey until it is all eaten. Tigers often hunt at night.

Most tigers avoid people as much as possible, but some become terrible human eaters. A human-eating tiger can terrify populations in dozens of square miles of countryside. People refuse to travel at night or go to remote villages. An unarmed person is no match for such a human eater. Tigers have even been known to raid villages, ripping through the thin walls and doors of houses to get at the people within.

Mammals—The Dangerous Cats   (3)

In 1911, the famous hunter and writer Jim Corbett killed an Indian tiger that had been a human eater for the previous eight years. This tiger was reported to have killed more than four hundred people in that time. Corbett said that most tigers that become human eaters are old or injured animals. The tigers turn to people as their prey because they are not able to catch swifter animals. Hunters sometimes wound a tiger and then fail to follow it and kill it. These tigers become even more dangerous to people. Even today, areas in India, Bangladesh, and Southeast Asia have trouble with tigers that have become human eaters.

4. Is the lion the "king of the jungle"?

The African lion doesn't even live in the jungle. Lions live on the large grassy plains that cover great areas of Africa. Lions are much more social animals than any of the other big cats. They usually hunt their prey in pairs or in groups called prides. The males of the pride parade in full view of a herd of grazing animals while one or more of the female lions quietly circle behind the herd. The lordly male lion with his magnificent mane does all the roaring while the female does all the killing. The lion is not the "king of the jungle," but you might call the lioness the "queen of the plains."

5. Do lions eat people?

Like tigers, lions are rarely human eaters, but this is not always true. In British East Africa (now Uganda) at the turn of the century, a number of lions terrorized the construction workers who were building a railroad. The lions killed so many of the workers that building was halted completely for weeks. At least twenty-eight of the Indian railway workers and unknown scores of Africans were killed; most of these poor victims were eaten.

Human-eating lions have appeared in many other places since that time, including Tanzania, South Africa, and Mozambique. In spite of all these accounts, it is still true that lions rarely bother people at all.

6. Is the black panther more dangerous than the leopard?

The black panther really is a leopard. If you look carefully at a black leopard in a zoo, you can even see the spots. Both the spotted and black varieties of the animal are called either leopards or panthers. The two different colors can even be seen in cubs from the same litter.

Adding to the confusion about names is the fact that in the Americas the mountain lion, or puma, is sometimes called a panther. But the puma is a different kind of cat from the leopard, black or spotted.

7. Why is the leopard, or panther, so dangerous?

Even though the leopard is small compared to the lion and the tiger, many people think that it is the most dangerous of the big cats. For its weight, the leopard is one of the strongest of the cats. It is an excellent climber and can run up a tree with astonishing speed. It can even climb a tree while carrying prey twice its own weight. It can leap up more than ten feet in the air and leap down on prey from a height of forty feet.

The leopard's skin of grayish gold with dark spots or rings provides excellent camouflage among the sun-dappled branches of a tree. Although the leopard may be about during the daylight, it is most active in the dark. The silent nighttime hunter will drop down on its quarry from a tree limb over a trail or overtake it in a few long leaps.

The leopard is particularly dangerous because it eats dogs, which may bring it near towns and villages. Leopards sometimes turn into deadly human eaters, terrorizing large areas for years. A leopard can easily carry a full-grown person off into the bushes or up a tree.

The late hunter Jim Corbett wrote about a leopard that killed four hundred people before he shot it in 1910. Corbett said that human-eating leopards are rare but very difficult to stop because they are so smart and so wary. Such leopards still appear from time to time in India and Africa. However, most leopards will not attack people unless provoked or wounded. And this beautiful cat will not survive long unless people stop killing it for its coat.

8. How dangerous is the jaguar?

The jaguar is the biggest cat in the Americas. It is found throughout South and Central America and Mexico. The jaguar preys on almost any animal it finds, including wild pigs, monkeys, the capybara (a giant rodent), and even alligators and turtles. The jaguar is a strong swimmer and an excellent climber. At night, the jaguar's deep, coughing roar sends shivers through the inhabitants of the jungle. No wonder they call the jaguar *el tigre* and avoid it whenever possible.

The jaguar can certainly be dangerous to people. But it seems to be more of a people killer than a people eater. While there are stories of jaguars eating people, most of the time they claw or kill people from anger rather than for food. Yet the jaguar is the only animal of the Americas that may become a people eater.

9. How dangerous is the puma, or mountain lion?

The puma is known by several other names, including mountain lion, cougar, and even panther. The puma is a graceful animal, six feet long and over one hundred pounds in weight. Its weird, drawn-out shriek is a wild and hair-raising sound in the North American wilderness.

The puma hunts big wild animals such as deer and sometimes elk. It will also kill domestic animals such as cattle, sheep, horses, and pigs. The very powerful puma is a silent tracker and a great jumper. It can drag an animal five times its own weight for a hundred yards.

Despite its ability to kill large animals, the puma rarely attacks people. True stories of pumas attacking humans are scarce. Pumas do cause some damage to livestock. But the real amount of damage is debatable. Many scientists feel that the puma is a natural check to the number of deer in an area and does little harm. But this does not seem to stop the puma hunters. The number of pumas is becoming smaller and smaller. It would be a great shame if this beautiful animal were to become extinct.

10. Which is the fastest of the dangerous cats?

The cheetah, sometimes called the hunting leopard, is the fastest land animal in the world. From a resting position, it can reach a speed of forty-five miles per hour in two seconds. In full stride, cheetahs have been clocked going over seventy miles per hour. After about four or five hundred yards, the cheetah slows down. However, if it is able to reach an antelope or other prey in that time, it can kill in a matter of seconds.

The cheetah is the most doglike of all the cats. It has long, slender legs and thick claws that are always unsheathed. Usually two or three cheetahs hunt together. At one time in India, cheetahs were tamed and used for hunting.

For all its speed and power, the cheetah normally is not dangerous to people. Cheetahs are not known for ever attacking people without being provoked. And even provoked attacks upon people are very rare and not usually fatal. In fact, people are far more dangerous to the beautifully furred cheetah than the other way around.

Dangerous Mammals–
Bears, Wolves, and
Wild Dogs

11. Are bears dangerous?

There are many different kinds of bears around the world. Some of them are very dangerous and apt to attack if you come near them. Others are less dangerous and will avoid people whenever possible. But all bears are very powerful animals and can be dangerous up close. Most people agree that the most dangerous bears include the polar bear, the brown bears (which include the grizzly bear and the Kodiak bear), the North American black bear, the Asian sloth bear, and the black bear of India.

Bears become more dangerous after they become adults. In the breeding season, bears become cranky and are more likely to attack people. Bears are very much individuals. What one bear does may not be the same as what another bear would do in the same situation. It is just not safe to go near a bear in the wild, not even one that seems to be very peaceful and used to people.

12. Do bears kill with a "bear hug"?

According to many fiction writers, bears attack by grabbing a victim and squeezing the person to death with the infamous "bear hug." The only trouble with these stories is that they probably never happened. Bears attack by using their sharp teeth to bite. They can also strike powerful blows with their front paws. But a bear attack usually happens as the bear is running on four legs, not standing up on its hind legs as a human fighter would. So the bear is in no position to "hug" someone.

13. Which is the biggest bear in the world?

The Kodiak bear, which lives on some islands in the Gulf of Alaska, is the largest meat-eating land animal in the world. Adult Kodiak bears weigh more than one thousand pounds and stand ten feet high. Second in size to the Kodiak is the peninsula giant bear of Alaska, which can also weigh close to one thousand pounds and stand eight feet high.

The big bears rarely go after large animals or people. The bears feed mostly on plants, insects, mice, and other small animals for much of the year. In June, when the salmon come up the rivers to spawn, the bears feast on the fish.

14. How dangerous are bears in national parks?

There is no doubt that grizzly bears or brown bears in national

parks can be very dangerous. The grizzly can be particularly dangerous. Although the grizzly is smaller than the Alaskan bears, it still weighs more than five hundred pounds and is from six to eight feet long. There are many true stories of grizzlies attacking and killing visitors to national parks. Not many years ago, grizzlies attacked and killed two visitors to Glacier National Park. Some people said that all the grizzlies in the parks had to be destroyed or moved away. Other people said that bears and people could still exist safely in the parks. They proposed new rules for visitors to the parks and for bear management. Troublesome bears, for example, are marked with yellow paint and may be destroyed if they continue to bother people.

Even though there is only a tiny chance of a bear attack in a national park, there are still some safety rules that all people should follow: Bears should never be fed from the windows of cars. And certainly people should never walk up to a bear for any reason whatsoever. This is particularly true in national parks, where bears get used to people and try to get food from them. Even a "friendly looking" bear may suddenly attack. If you follow the rules about not feeding bears, storing food properly, and discarding garbage, then you'll not only make it safer for people but for the bears, as well.

While it is true that bears in national parks can be dangerous, it is also true that more people are injured and killed in boating accidents, in swimming, in climbing, in fishing, and in most other activities than by bears. And it is difficult to imagine people saying that no one can swim in a lake because someone once drowned there. And just as there is no reason one cannot swim in a lake because someone drowned there, there is no reason to avoid national parks because of the bears.

15. How dangerous are wolves?

Like other meat eaters, wolves prey on other animals. Wolves are powerful hunting animals. In North America, they can weigh up to one hundred seventy-five pounds. Wolves hunt alone, in small groups, or in large packs. A pack of wolves can bring down large wild animals such as the caribou, moose, or bison. Wolves can also attack domestic animals such as sheep and cattle.

So wolves are certainly capable of attacks on unarmed human beings. Wolves have a very bad reputation. Many stories are told of ferocious attacks upon people. The "big bad wolf" is even a creature of legend. But there are some odd things about these wolf stories. Most of the stories date back to earlier times, and only a few of them come from North America. Even in the 1800s, when there were many wolves in the American West, only rarely were there true reports of attacks on people.

In fact, during one twenty-five-year period, the United States Fish and Wildlife Service could not verify a single reported unprovoked wolf attack on people. So what is the answer to the question, Is the wolf dangerous to people or not?

The answer is that the wolf may not be as dangerous as was once thought. There is a strong possibility that much of what has been written about the wolf is fiction and not fact. The true story of the wolf is only now being told, but the wolf does not look nearly so bad as it once did.

Within their own families, wolves are far from bloodthirsty killers. Male and female often remain together for life. The mother and the father both care for the cubs. Wolves are highly social animals. They have a whole variety of facial expressions and sounds that they use to communicate with one another. Some scientists even claim to be able to communicate with wolves in their own "language."

Wolves are now rare and hardly dangerous to people. If attacks on people did take place in the past, they were probably much fewer in number than the many stories would have you believe. Wolves usually prey on weak or dying animals and keep wild animal populations from becoming too large. But they are slowly becoming extinct, and it would be a shame if they ever vanish altogether.

16. Are there any dangerous wild dogs?

The African or Cape hunting dog roams in the bush country south of the Sahara Desert. Hunting in packs of a dozen or more, the dogs are able to bring down antelopes and other large game. The packs are continually on the move after food and travel great distances in their search.

The Cape hunting dog can reach the size of a large domestic dog or a small wolf. It has long legs, powerful jaws in a big head, and a bushy tail. It looks something like a hyena with its large, upright ears.

There are only a few reports of these hunting dogs attacking people. Like wolves, the dogs are becoming fewer in number as people begin to encroach on their hunting grounds. The dogs are in far more danger *from* people than they are a danger *to* people.

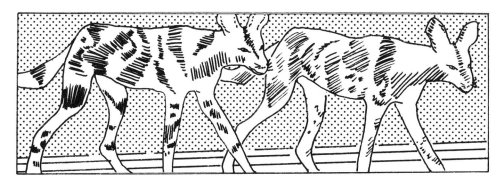

17. Is the coyote dangerous to humans and livestock?

The coyote is widely hunted by sheepherders. It is shot at, snared, and poisoned. Some people think that the coyote kills much livestock—that it is a menace that should be exterminated. But the bad reputation of the coyote is mostly undeserved.

Wildlife scientists have studied the coyote's food habits very closely. The coyote never harms people directly. And it kills only a small fraction of the livestock that it is blamed for. Coyotes eat mostly rats, mice, rabbits, prairie dogs, and ground squirrels. All of these animals eat grass. Sheep eat grass, too. Thus, the coyote does more good as a destroyer of small grass-eating animals than harm as a killer of livestock.

18. How dangerous is the laughing hyena?

Hyenas are hunters of live animals as well as feeders upon the dead. The spotted hyena is active at night and is much feared by people in Africa and India. Every few years there are newspaper accounts of hyenas attacking young children in these places. There are also legends and stories about bloodthirsty hyenas that attack unsuspecting people in their sleep.

But chances are that these stories are exaggerated and that the hyena has been blamed for what some other animal did. Still, the hyena can be dangerous and undoubtedly sometimes attacks children or weakened adults.

Hyenas are powerful hunting animals. A full-grown spotted hyena may weigh up to one hundred seventy-five pounds and be three feet high at its shoulders. It has a broad face and powerful jaws and teeth. It can crack a bone between its teeth with ease. It has great strength in its heavy legs. The hyena is no laughing matter.

19. Are foxes and jackals dangerous?

The jackal and the fox have the reputation of being smart and sneaky. These animals might be dangerous if you cornered them or tried to handle them. They certainly can bite. But there is no evidence that foxes or jackals normally attack people.

20. Are wolverines, weasels, or badgers dangerous?

As with jackals and foxes, all these animals are capable of giving a nasty bite if cornered. But again, normally they will not attack people.

(3)

Dangerous Mammals– Monkeys and Apes

21. Are gorillas dangerous?

The gorilla is the largest of the great apes. A big male gorilla weighs as much as six hundred pounds and has a chest five feet around. Its great arms hang down to the middle of its legs when the gorilla stands erect.

In spite of its enormous strength and strong teeth, the gorilla is not dangerous unless attacked. In fact, the gorilla has no natural enemies in the forests where it lives. Sometimes the male head of a family group will rise to his feet and beat his breast like a drum to warn off human intruders. But a gorilla will only attack in rare cases. Usually, gorillas will avoid people whenever possible. At the first sign of a person, a troop of gorillas will often melt into the forest and disappear. The stories about gorillas kidnapping women or children are just fables—there is no truth to them.

22. Is there a dangerous humanlike ape in the world?

There are many tales of "ape men" from around the world. Perhaps the most famous of these are the stories of the abominable snowman, or *yeti*, of the Himalayas and Bigfoot of the American Northwest. But there is simply no substantial proof that any humanlike ape exists. The gorilla, the chimpanzee, and the orang-utan are the only great apes that even come close to being humanlike, and none of them are found in the wild in the Himalayas or in the northwestern United States.

23. Is the orang-utan dangerous?

The orang-utan is a big, powerful animal. A full-grown orang male can weigh two hundred pounds and has an arm spread greater than that of a gorilla. An orang is an intelligent animal and extremely strong.

Like the gorilla, the orang will not attack humans unless bothered or threatened by them. When it is confronted by a person, it is more likely to disappear into the forest than it is to attack. That doesn't mean that it would be safe for you to try to touch an orang in captivity or in a zoo. Its great strength makes it too dangerous for such close contact.

The orang-utan lives in the forests of Borneo and Sumatra. Its name is from the Malay language and means "man of the woods." Like the gorilla, the orang has no natural enemies in its native home.

24. Are chimpanzees dangerous?

Chimpanzees are intelligent, strong animals. Chimps behave very differently one from another. Young chimps can be affectionate with people and may lead you to believe that any chimp can be played with. But that's not so. Some chimps, particularly older males, can be bad tempered. A large chimp can easily bite or injure a person who comes too close. Of course, an attack by a chimp is much more likely in a zoo or circus than in the wild. Like all the other great apes, chimps usually don't attack people in the wild unless threatened or bothered.

25. Are there any dangerous monkeys?

Many kinds of large monkeys are capable of giving a person a nasty bite. For example, rhesus monkeys in India are allowed to roam free because of their special place in the Hindu religion. Because of their familiarity with people, these monkeys sometimes attack and bite people, children in particular. But most monkeys are shy and quite harmless unless they are bothered or attacked.

There is one kind of monkey that can be very dangerous and even kill people. This dangerous monkey is the baboon. Baboons are very powerful and have large teeth. They are also very intelligent and social. They live in large troops and will mass-attack even a hunting leopard. Baboons sometimes raid farms and homes in Africa and Asia and kill sheep or other domestic animals for food. Baboons have even been known to steal human infants. Baboon troops should always be given a wide berth.

(4)

Dangerous Mammals–
Killer Whales and
Other Sea Animals

26. Are killer whales the most dangerous
sea animals?

Many people think that killer whales are the most dangerous animals in the sea. There is no doubt that they are great hunters of other sea animals. Killer whales feed on seals, penguins, porpoises, and dolphins. Packs of them have been known to attack and kill larger whales, even the giant blue whale.

Killer whales are the largest dolphins in the world. Their black and white coloring may remind you of the coloring of a penguin. An adult male killer may be thirty feet long and weigh nine tons. Yet despite their size, they can propel their streamlined bodies clear out of the water with a flip of their muscular tails.

An adult killer whale has as many as fifty three-inch-long teeth, which curve inward and interlock when the whale closes its mouth. The teeth are used for ripping and tearing food, not for chewing. Food animals are swallowed whole or in huge chunks.

The killer whale is certainly capable of being dangerous to humans. And there are a number of stories that tell of killer whale attacks upon people. The curious thing is that most of these stories don't stand up to close investigation. Often the animal in the stories turns out to be a shark, such as the great white shark. Actually, there have been very few proven accounts of killer whales attacking people.

Sea scientists are divided in their opinions about the killer whale. Many feel that the stories about killer whale attacks upon people are just fanciful tales made up by newspaper or magazine writers. Others think that some of the tales may be at least partly true. Perhaps most scientists would agree that the killer whale is not likely to go after people. But they also think that if someone were to fall into the sea near a hungry or excited killer whale, there is a chance that the whale would attack.

To people who have seen killer whales in large aquariums, the "cruel" killer may have become the "friendly" whale. Yet the killer whale has not changed. It hunts other animals for food. In following its nature, it is neither good nor bad. It is just one part of the natural order of living things in the sea.

27. Are sperm whales dangerous to sailors in small boats?

Sperm whales are sixty- to eighty-foot giants that were once found in all the seas around the world. Perhaps the most famous sperm whale is the fictional Moby Dick in Melville's classic book. Although normally not likely to bother people, sperm whales will sometimes turn on their pursuers during a hunt. Wounded sperm whales used their mighty heads as battering rams to crush the hull of more than one wooden whaling ship.

But the sperm whale has been harmed by people more than it has harmed people. The sperm whale is too valuable to whalers for its own good and has been hunted close to extinction. Recently, most whaling nations have agreed to limit the hunting of this unique animal. Perhaps the sperm whale may yet be saved from destruction.

28. Are there any dangerous seals?

Leopard seals are fierce sea hunters. A large male may be ten feet long and weigh over six hundred pounds. Leopard seals have powerful jaws fitted with long, pointed teeth that curve inward. They use their teeth for ripping at their prey.

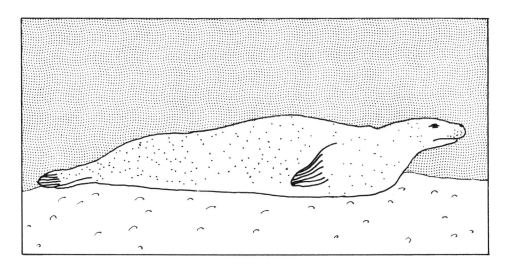

Leopard seals are also very swift, excellent swimmers. The seals live in Antarctic waters, where they feed on penguins and other kinds of seals. There are stories of leopard seals chasing explorers across the ice, but these are just fiction. There has never been any true account of a leopard seal trying to make a meal of a person.

29. Are walruses dangerous?

Walruses are large sea animals. A male walrus can weigh a ton and a half. It also has two large tusks with which to attack an enemy. But a walrus couldn't have much interest in a person as a food animal. Walruses eat mostly shellfish, and the majority of their teeth are rounded for crushing shells. Of course, it would not be a great idea for you to get too close to this huge animal, particularly during its breeding season. But other than that, walruses are not dangerous to people.

30. Are there any other dangerous sea mammals?

Many seals and sea lions have sharp teeth and can give you a nasty bite if you come too close and bother them. Some of these animals become very aggressive during their breeding season and will attack if you intrude on their territory. But most scientists agree that normally these animals will not attack a person. As for dolphins, porpoises, and other sea mammals, none are known to have attacked people, and they are not considered dangerous.

(5)

Other Dangerous Mammals

31. How dangerous is the rhinoceros?

The rhinoceros is the second or third largest of all land mammals; the hippo vies with the rhino for second place behind the elephant. A black rhino can weigh one and a half tons when full-grown. The white or square-lipped rhino is the biggest of all the rhinos. It stands six and a half feet tall at the shoulder and can weigh up to four tons.

The rhino is protected by a thick, tough hide. Its huge head has either one or two horns, depending upon the species. The horn is actually not a bone at all. It is an outgrowth of closely matted hair and skin. The front horn on the African black rhino (it has two horns) can reach a length of four feet.

Rhinos are plant eaters. They feed mostly on the tender leaves of low bushes and grasses. They are very nearsighted and have short tempers. A rhino may rush forward in a fierce attack for no apparent reason. Sometimes, they will even charge a car or a truck and batter it or overturn it. But often they will charge and then turn aside at the last moment.

Of course, a rhino can be very dangerous. Anyone in the way

of a rhino charge, accidentally or otherwise, very likely would be gored by a horn or trampled to death. Over the years, many people have been killed or injured by getting too close to a rhino and unwittingly provoking a charge. It makes sense for people to avoid rhinos unless they are with a guide who is well versed in rhino behavior.

32. Is the hippopotamus dangerous?

Hippos don't look particularly dangerous on land, but in the water they can be killers. A herd of hippos may submerge or scatter when people in a boat come near. But it is also possible that the boat may be struck, sunk, and the people in it attacked and killed. As with rhinos, it is best for people to avoid hippos unless they are with a guide who knows the hippos' habits.

Hippos are fast swimmers. They have large teeth that can rip through an alligator's armored skin with one bite. A yawning hippo is not about to fall asleep. It is actually warning off other hippos that are intruding. If the intruder doesn't leave, a giant fight may break out.

The name *hippopotamus* comes from a Greek word that means "river horse." The large, ungainly word is just right for this large, ungainly animal. A hippo can weigh up to four tons and have a head and body length of twelve feet. A full-grown hippo's head can weigh nearly a ton! Except for a few hairs on its head and tail, the hippo's skin is mostly hairless.

33. Are wild pigs dangerous?

Many kinds of wild pigs are dangerous. The wild boar of Europe and Asia is the largest and probably the most dangerous of its kind. A large boar weighs more than three hundred pounds and has a head and body length of five feet. Its large, sharp tusks may be almost a foot long.

In the past, boar hunting was a sport in many parts of Europe and Asia. When at bay, the boar was more than a match for a pack of dogs. The boar would charge at mounted or unmounted hunters, often wounding or killing them.

34. Are there any dangerous wild pigs in the Americas?

The peccaries are dangerous piglike animals that live in both North and South America. The peccaries are not true pigs, although they resemble them closely. The collared peccary lives in the south-western United States and all the way south down to the tip of South America.

A peccary is a fierce animal when attacked and easily able to injure or even kill an unarmed human. There are stories of packs of peccaries chasing people up trees and keeping them treed for hours. There are also reports of peccaries attacking people on horses and ripping at the horses' legs. Wild pigs and peccaries will not come looking for people, but they certainly can be dangerous to approach.

35. How dangerous are wild elephants?

Elephants are plant eaters, not people eaters. Usually, if left alone, elephants will not bother people. But there is no doubt that the elephant can be extremely dangerous to hunters and others who bother them. Elephants have enormous strength and great speed; a charging elephant moves at twenty miles or more an hour. No one could survive a really determined elephant attack. Many experts consider the elephant the most dangerous animal in the world to hunt.

The African elephant is the largest land animal in the world. It can reach a shoulder height of thirteen feet and weigh over six tons. Each ear can be four feet wide, and the spread across the stretched-out ears and head can be ten feet. An elephant's tusks can each be over eight feet long and weigh more than two hundred pounds. The African elephant, not the lion, is truly the "king of beasts."

36. Can elephants be dangerous to people who are not hunters?

The elephant's huge appetite sometimes makes it dangerous to people. Elephants eat four or five hundred pounds of food every day. Of course, this food is all plants and not people. But an elephant's food habits can make it dangerous in another way. Elephants travel widely in their search for food. In their travels, the elephants sometimes come across farms and eat the crops.

A herd of wild elephants can feed on and trample the crops on many acres of farmland in a single day. Farmers who are inexperienced with elephants can easily be harmed or killed if they try to drive the elephants away. A herd of wild elephants fears nothing in the world and, if bothered, will attack anything in sight, including people, cars, and even houses.

37. Are there any poisonous mammals?

Most people know that there are poisonous snakes and other reptiles. Some people know that there are poisonous fish. But few people know that there are also poisonous mammals. Scientists say that there are only two groups of poisonous mammals in the world.

One group of poisonous mammals is the primitive egg-laying mammals of Australia, called monotremes. The duck-billed platypus is the best known of the monotremes. On the inside of the male platypus's legs are spurs that have tubes leading up the legs to poison glands in the body. These spurs work the same way as the fangs of poisonous snakes. They are the only means of defense that the male platypus has. The spurs can be driven deep into flesh with a slashing stroke. The poisonous wound can be serious to a person handling a platypus, but otherwise the platypus is of no danger to people.

The other group of poisonous animals is the smallest mammals in the world—the shrews. The largest shrew is about the size of a mouse; the smaller ones weigh only about as much as a penny. Shrews, which eat mostly insects and other rodents, have to eat almost constantly in order to stay alive. A shrew would starve to death in a few hours without food.

The American short-tailed shrew has glands that make a poison very similar to that of a cobra. When the shrew bites, the poison flows along a path on the teeth and into the wound. The poison can kill something as small as a mouse but can do little harm to anything the size of a human being. And the idea of a shrew attack on a person is silly. Shrews really are not dangerous to people.

38. Are bats dangerous?

Despite what you may have been told, most bats are really no danger to people. Many kinds of bats might give you a good bite if you were to handle them, but so might your pet cat or dog. About the only bats that might be dangerous are the blood-lapping vampire bats of the tropics.

Vampire bats actually feed on the blood of other animals, from small ones to cattle to humans. The cuts they make with their teeth are small, and the amount of blood they take is not large. But while the idea of having your blood lapped up by a vampire bat is

rather disgusting, the bat itself can do little harm. What might be dangerous is the disease germs that the bat can carry, including the deadly ones that cause rabies.

Rabid animals of any kind (all mammals can carry rabies) can be of great danger. Any wild mammal (or domestic one, for that matter) that bites a human can transmit rabies. The rabid animal should be killed or safely captured and brought to the nearest hospital or doctor. Rabies is a disease that *must* be treated. It will not go away. Untreated cases of rabies almost always cause death.

39. Which is the most dangerous rodent?

There are five thousand different kinds of rodents—a large group of gnawing animals. They are found all over the world in almost every imaginable habitat. Most rodents reproduce so rapidly that their populations are enormous unless controlled by some natural enemy or by lack of food. Many rodents can be problems, but the most dangerous rodent by far is the rat. Rats alone account for hundreds of millions of dollars of crop damage each year. Rats also kill thousands of baby chicks, ducks, and geese every night of the year. They also injure and kill baby pigs, lambs, and other domestic animals.

Rats are dangerous to people, too, particularly to infants. Many reports are made each year of infants being attacked and bitten in their cribs and beds. Some of the babies even die of their wounds. There are probably many more unreported rat attacks on people.

If you total up the amount of attacks on people, the amount of food and money lost, and the amount of trouble, then the rat is the most dangerous wild mammal in the world. Rats have to be kept constantly under control or they will destroy crops, kill domestic animals, and seriously threaten the food supply of the world.

Compared to rats, the other rodents are only pests. They can give a nasty bite if handled carelessly, but few will deliberately attack a person.

40. What are some other dangerous mammals?

The buffalo of Africa (not the bison of North America and Europe that are mistakenly called buffalo) can be very dangerous animals. The black or Cape buffalo is a large, powerful animal with great curved horns that may measure seven feet from tip to tip.

When this great buffalo charges like an express train, it is almost impossible to stop except with a skillfully aimed bullet. The buffalo has a short temper and will attack anyone who comes too close. Some hunters consider the Cape buffalo to be the most dangerous game animal in Africa, even more dangerous to hunt than the elephant, lion, and rhinoceros.

The water buffalo of southern Asia is also a powerful and short-tempered animal. There are a number of reports of these buffalo attacking and injuring people. The gaur, a wild ox found in India and Southeast Asia, is another animal that will attack a person and can seriously injure anyone it hits.

Other mammals may be dangerous in certain situations. For example, a large male deer or moose or elk may chase and even injure a person who comes too close, particularly during the breeding season. In fact, any large wild animal may be dangerous when it turns to fight if it is injured or cornered.

(6)

Dangerous Birds

41. Can an eagle carry off a baby?

There are many old tales and legends about eagles carrying off babies and even small children. There was even an old movie that supposedly showed an eagle carrying a small child off to its nest. The special effects in the movie were not believable; you could see that the eagle was just a stuffed bird. And the old tales are just as unbelievable; an eagle would find it very difficult to carry any object that weighs as much as a child. Eagles attack and can carry small rodents, snakes, fish, and smaller birds. But there are no known cases where an eagle has stolen a child and flown off with it.

As a matter of fact, eagles rarely, if ever, will attack a person. Even when someone climbs up to an eagle's nest, the eagle will fly around in excitement but usually will not attack. If anything, eagles are shy and will avoid people whenever possible.

42. Are hawks and falcons dangerous?

Falcons and hawks are birds that prey on other birds. These hunters of the sky are swift enough to catch their prey in midair. A peregrine falcon has been timed at sixty miles per hour in straight flight and more than eighty miles per hour in a dive. Falcons and hawks are also well fitted to hunt in other ways. They have strong, hooked beaks; curved claws, or talons; and extraordinarily keen eyes.

An adult falcon or hawk certainly could inflict serious injury if it ever dived down to attack a person. And it is possible that people who have disturbed these birds or attempted to rob their nests may have been injured in attacks. But there are few stories of a falcon or hawk attacking a person for no reason. The injuries that these birds sometimes cause are usually to people who are training them for the sport of falconry.

43. Are vultures dangerous?

Vultures are very large birds that often exceed even eagles in size. For example, the bearded vulture stands nearly four feet tall and has a wingspread of close to ten feet. Vultures feed upon the bodies of dead animals. Flocks of a dozen or more may assemble to devour the remains of a large mammal. If you were to walk into a flock of feeding vultures, they might very well run at you. But for the most part, vultures do not attack people—at least not while the people are alive.

44. Are ostriches dangerous?

Ostriches are the largest birds in the world. Adult ostriches are seven or eight feet tall and weigh up to three hundred pounds or more. Ostriches have excellent vision and can run at a good forty miles per hour.

Perhaps you have heard the story that an ostrich will bury its head in the sand when confronted by danger. The story is just a fable. An ostrich will kick viciously when cornered or angry. Its large clawed legs can hit with the force of a heavyweight boxer's best knockdown punch. An angry ostrich also seems to be without fear and will continue to press its attack.

There are a number of true stories of ostriches attacking and injuring people. Because ostriches run around freely on game preserves, they often come into contact with people. The birds are also farmed in some places. And an angry ostrich will attack a person even when the person is on horseback.

But ostriches usually will not attack a person. Experts say that in the unlikely event that you are attacked by an ostrich, the best thing to do is to fall flat on the ground. It seems that even an excited ostrich will not step on you if you're lying flat!

45. Are birds dangerous to airplanes?

Birds actually are of some danger to people in planes. Each year there are a number of reports of birds colliding with planes in flight. Sometimes the planes are only slightly damaged. (The birds, of course, do not survive the collision.) But there are a few instances where planes have crashed and passengers have died as a result of colliding with a bird.

Birds can be a danger, not only in midair, but also in takeoffs and landings. The naval air base on Midway Island in the Pacific once had troubles with thousands of gooney birds, a kind of large albatross. The birds perched on the planes and sometimes ran into the propellers. Within a few months, they had caused ten plane crashes.

46. Are there any other dangerous birds?

Some birds have been known to attack people on occasion. The mute swan, for example, will attack anyone who comes too close to its nest. The bird swings at the intruder with its wings and can deliver a powerful blow. There are a few stories about young children approaching these birds' nests and being attacked and killed.

The skua is a bird of the cold regions of the Antarctic that preys on young penguins. It will also attack anyone coming too close to its nest. It could certainly deliver an injury with its sharp beak.

Anyone who handles pet birds should be prepared to be bitten from time to time. And some of these bites, such as those from parrots, can be very painful. But generally birds are no danger to people.

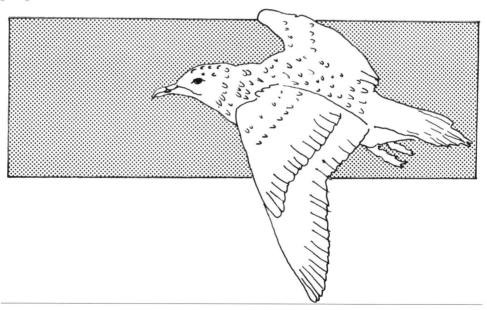

Dangerous Birds   (41)

(7)

Giant Snakes

47. How large are the giant snakes?

The giant snakes are the longest land animals in the world. They are even longer than the giraffe is tall. Giant snakes range in size from about twenty feet long (about as long as a car) to over thirty-five feet long (about as long as a school bus).

There are six giants of the snake world. The biggest snakes are the anaconda, the reticulated python, and the African python. The mid-sized giant snakes are the amethystine python and the Indian python. The smallest of the giant snakes is the boa constrictor, which is about eighteen to twenty feet long.

48. Are giant snakes dangerous?

All of the giant snakes kill by squeezing, or constricting, their prey. The snake grabs an animal with its teeth and then wraps itself around its prey and begins to squeeze. The constrictors don't actually crush an animal to death. What happens is that the animal cannot breathe, and it dies of suffocation in a few minutes.

Attacks by giant snakes on people are rare, but enough attacks are reported to prove that giant snakes can be dangerous and can even kill. While the snakes will sometimes attack people, they almost never try to eat them. Most people are just too large for a giant snake to swallow.

An attack by a giant snake makes the news around the world no matter where it happens. The fact that there are so few stories about these attacks just shows how rare they are.

49. Which giant snakes are the most dangerous?

The pythons seem to be the giant snakes that attack people the most. The reason probably is that pythons are not particularly rare and live in and around areas where people live. For example, pythons are found along busy waterways and even in large cities in Southeast Asia such as Bangkok. A python may attack a person because it has mistaken the person for an animal that it normally eats.

One story of a python attack comes from the city of Durban in South Africa. It seems that a gardener had a huge python unexpectedly drop on him from a tree. The gardener was understandably surprised, but he fought back against the snake and was finally able to free himself of the snake's coils without injury.

Other stories do not end so happily. On an Indonesian island, a woman was killed and swallowed by a reticulated python. In another case, a Malay boy of fifteen was killed and swallowed by a reticulated python. In still another case, a young woman washing clothes near a stream was attacked by an African python fourteen

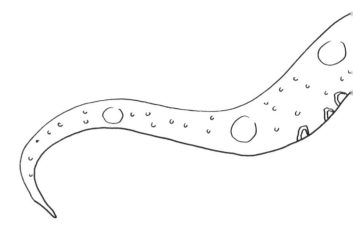

feet long and nearly one and a half feet wide. A man came by and saw the woman in the snake's coils. He called for help, but it was too late. The woman was dead by the time other people came and were able to kill the snake.

Stories are also told of attacks on people by anacondas. The anaconda is the biggest snake in the world. Anacondas are found in the tropical parts of South America. They live mostly in swamps and near lakes and slow-moving rivers. Anacondas hunt land animals such as pigs and rodents. But they are also good swimmers. They catch and eat water animals such as fish, turtles, even crocodiles.

One anaconda attacked a thirteen-year-old boy near his village. The boy disappeared from sight while swimming in a river. His companions saw bubbles rising from under the water. One dived down to investigate and felt the body of a snake below the water. The others called for help, and the snake was found and shot. The boy's body was recovered nearby.

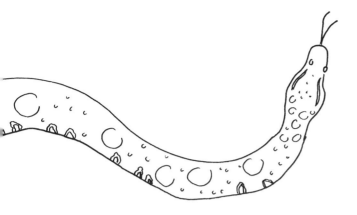

50. Are there any one-hundred-foot-long snakes in the world?

Over the years there have been many stories and reports of monster snakes one hundred feet in length and even longer. Most of the stories are just hard to believe. For example, in 1948, a newspaper in Brazil published a story of a giant anaconda one hundred fifty-six feet long. According to the newspaper account, the monster knocked down buildings and destroyed automobiles before it was finally killed by the army. Even nowadays you may see monster snakes in movies or read about them in books. But there has never been any proof that such huge snakes really exist.

Once, a well-known scientist offered a reward for anyone who could bring him an anaconda skin that was over forty feet in length. No one ever claimed the reward. The largest snake ever measured in the field was a thirty-seven-foot anaconda found in a river in South America.

(8)

Poisonous Snakes

51. Are all snakes poisonous?

Most snakes are not poisonous and are really quite harmless. Of the twenty-seven-hundred different kinds of snakes in the world, only about four hundred are poisonous. And of all the poisonous snakes, only about half that number are really dangerous to people.

52. Can you tell a poisonous snake by the shape of its head?

There is really no way that you can tell a poisonous snake from a nonpoisonous one just by looking at its head or body shape. It is just not true that all poisonous snakes have heavy, triangular heads and small, narrow eyes. Rattlesnakes look like that, but the very poisonous mambas and coral snakes have slender heads and round eyes. There are also some harmless snakes with heavy heads and bodies, such as the hog-nosed snake, that are sometimes mistaken for poisonous snakes.

Two kinds of snakes, the coral snake and the scarlet king snake, that live in North America look almost alike. Both have almost the same red, yellow, and black rings, and both are about the same size. Yet the coral snake has a venom that is very dangerous to people. The scarlet king is nonpoisonous and quite harmless.

53. How many people die of snakebite each year?

In the United States, there are only about one dozen cases of fatal snakebites each year. Mexico has about ten times that many. India has the highest number of fatal snakebites of any country in the world—from fifteen to twenty *thousand* deaths each year.

It is impossible to know exactly how many people die each year from poisonous snakebites. Many areas that abound in poisonous snakes keep few records. But some experts think that in the whole world there are about thirty to forty thousand deaths each year from snakebite.

54. How dangerous are poisonous snakes compared to other animals?

Poisonous snakes are more dangerous than bears, wolves, the big cats, sharks, elephants, and killer whales all put together. In fact, snakes are more dangerous than any other group of animals except, perhaps, insects. Snakes kill more people in a single year than sharks do in one hundred years; they kill more people in a single *month* than wolves and bears do in hundreds of years; they kill more people in a single *day* than killer whales have ever done.

55. If poisonous snakes are so dangerous, why don't we kill them all?

Poisonous snakes that come into areas where people live have to be killed. After all, no one wants to meet a poisonous snake on the way home from school or work. But poisonous snakes, even deadly ones, are far more likely to kill and eat rodents than to bite people. Poisonous snakes probably kill millions upon millions of rodents each year.

If we were to kill all the poisonous snakes, the rodents would greatly increase in number. Rodents eat food crops and spread disease. There would be more human death and suffering because of food shortages and the spread of disease than the snakes could ever cause.

Things are never simple in nature. There are no "good guys" or "bad guys." Poisonous snakes harm people in one way but help people in another way. Poisonous snakes (and nonpoisonous snakes) help to maintain the balance of nature—and that is good for all living things.

56. Where do rattlesnakes live?

Rattlesnakes are found all over the United States except for Maine and Delaware (where they seem to have been exterminated). Most rattlesnake bites occur in Arizona, Florida, Georgia, Texas, and Alabama. Rattlesnakes live in many different habitats, from prairies and plains to mountains and from deserts to forests. The southwest United States and northwest Mexico have more different kinds of rattlers than are found any other place.

Rattlesnakes get their name from the rattle at the end of the snake's tail. The rattle is a bell-shaped, hollow scale. Rattlesnakes can have as many as a dozen rattles, but after that the end of the tail usually breaks off. When the tail is shaken, the rattles hit against each other and make a noise. The noise is very loud, and a large rattler can be heard one hundred feet away. The rattle seems to be used to warn enemies away.

The eastern diamondback rattlesnake is the largest poisonous snake in the United States. It can reach a length of over eight feet and have fangs an inch long. The western diamondback is not quite as large but is much more numerous. This western diamondback is the snake responsible for more serious bites and deaths than is any other snake in North America. Other rattlers in the United States include the sidewinder, the timber, the prairie, the massasauga, and the pygmy. The latter two snakes are less than two feet long and only slightly poisonous.

57. Which cobras are the most dangerous?

The king cobra is the largest poisonous snake in the world. A few king cobras reach a length of eighteen feet, but most adults are about fourteen feet long. Many snake experts think that the king cobra is the most dangerous snake in the world. Its venom is powerful enough to kill an elephant. The snake is very aggressive, particularly during its mating season. The king cobra lives in Southeast Asia, India, and southern China.

The common or Indian cobra is also a deadly snake. It is about one-third the size of the king cobra. It is much more commonly

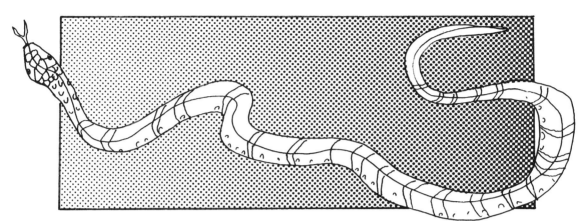

found in populated areas than is the king cobra, and is therefore far more likely to come in contact with people and bite them. The Indian cobra has one of the largest hoods of any of the cobras. The hood is formed by the snake raising and pushing the long ribs behind its neck. The skin stretches across the ribs, forming a hood four times as wide as the snake's body. The Indian cobra ranges all over India, the Philippines, and Southeast Asia.

Two African cobras, the ringhals and the black-necked cobra, are known as spitting cobras. They can squirt jets of venom through their fangs a distance of six to ten feet. Usually, the venom that hits the eyes of a person is not enough to kill, but it does cause severe pain and sometimes even blindness. These cobras can spit up to twenty jets of venom at a time, one jet right after another.

58. Are there any poisonous sea snakes?

All of the fifty different kinds of sea snakes are poisonous. Their fangs and venom are very much like those of the cobras. Most sea snakes are found in the warm coastal waters of the western Pacific and Indian oceans. They feed on fish, which they hunt at any time of the day or night.

Sea snakes have a powerful venom. One kind of sea snake has a venom fifty times more poisonous than that of the king cobra. Sea snakes generally don't come into contact with people other than fishermen. Sea snakes rarely bite a person. Bathers, for example, are never attacked by sea snakes in the area. Even so, sea snakes can be dangerous if captured or touched by anyone who isn't expert at handling them.

59. What are some dangerous African snakes?

The black mamba is the largest African poisonous snake and the one that people fear most. The black mamba usually is about ten feet long, but some are longer than fourteen feet. It is a slender, fast-moving snake that strikes quickly and has a deadly nerve venom. The green mamba is smaller and much less dangerous than the black mamba.

The puff adder lives all over Africa except in the rain forests. Many live in the dry semidesert regions. The puff adder puffs itself up and hisses a warning when it is alarmed. It strikes very quickly, either forward or sideways. Its poison is slow acting but can still cause death.

The Gaboon viper lives in the rain forests of central Africa. It has a heavy, wide body and a head larger than your fist. This six-foot-long snake has two-inch-long fangs and very powerful venom. But reports of bites from this snake are rare. It seems the snake

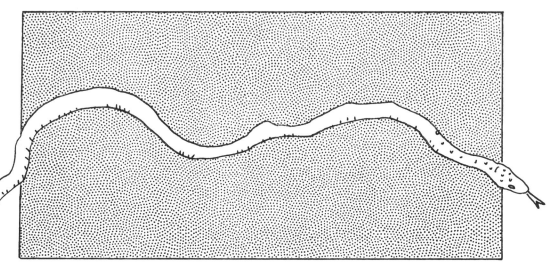

hisses, flattens its body, and makes short lunges at anyone who comes too close. That's enough to chase most people away before they get bitten. But if this snake does bite, death often follows quickly.

The rhinoceros viper is closely related to the puff adder and the Gaboon viper. It lives in the swampy areas of central Africa. It has a powerful poison and is much feared there.

60. What are some other poisonous snakes from around the world?

The taipan of Australia is one of the most deadly snakes in the world. It grows to a length of more than ten feet. When it bites, it can inject a large amount of highly poisonous nerve venom. Anyone bitten by a taipan will probably die in a few minutes. The only reason the taipan doesn't kill many people is that it lives in areas of northeast Australia that are only lightly populated.

The death adder and the tiger snake are two other highly poisonous snakes of Australia. Australia, in fact, is the only continent where poisonous snakes outnumber the nonpoisonous ones. Forty to fifty percent of people bitten by the death adder or the tiger snake die. That puts these snakes high on the list of the most dangerous snakes in the world.

The bushmaster of Central and South America is also one of the most dangerous snakes in the world. This large snake, over twelve feet in length, is very poisonous and often attacks people for no apparent reason. It has enough venom to kill several people at one time.

The fer-de-lance is a smaller poisonous snake that lives in the same area as the bushmaster. Its venom is deadly and fast acting. Also, it is even more likely to bite than is the bushmaster.

The water moccasin, or cottonmouth, is found in the southeastern United States, mainly Mississippi and Florida. Its poison is about as powerful as that of a rattler and can cause death. The much smaller copperhead is found in the eastern United States from Florida to New England. Its bite is not as deadly as the water moccasin's.

Coral snakes live in North and South America. Their venom is highly poisonous, but a coral snake's teeth are small and it rarely bites people. However, when a coral snake does bite, its venom often causes death.

There are many other poisonous snakes that can cause pain and even death. The ones mentioned in this chapter are those that experts think are the most dangerous.

(9)

Dangerous Reptiles

61. Are alligators the same as crocodiles?

Crocodiles and alligators, along with the smaller caimans and gavials, belong to one group of animals, called crocodilians. All the crocodilians are reptiles that look pretty much alike except for some minor differences. For example, a crocodile's head narrows from the eyes to the tip of the snout. When a crocodile closes its jaws, one or two large teeth in the lower jaw are completely exposed. That's what makes a crocodile look as though it's grinning. Some grin! In contrast, an alligator's head is almost as broad at the tip of the snout as it is at the eyes. And when an alligator closes its jaws, the teeth in the lower jaw are not visible.

The crocodilians are cousins of the giant reptiles of millions of years ago. Nowadays, at least as far as weight is concerned, the crocodilians are the largest living reptiles. Some kinds of crocodiles average fifteen feet long and weigh more than one ton. There have even been reports of crocodiles measuring more than twenty-five feet and weighing as much as three tons!

62. How do crocodilians attack people?

All crocodilians live in the water, where they eat any animal that comes by, from a fish to a person. Crocodilians cannot chew. If their prey is too large to swallow in one gulp, they have to tear it apart. Sometimes they drag large animals (and people) below the surface until their prey drowns.

Once the animals are dead, or even before, the crocodilians begin to tear the body apart. The crocs clamp down with their jaws on an arm or a leg. Then they use their powerful tails to spin in the water, ripping the arm or leg off. In a short time, the crocs have dismembered the body and fed. If any part of the body is left after a croc satisfies its hunger, the remains may be brought back to a den of youngsters in a nearby bank of the river or lake.

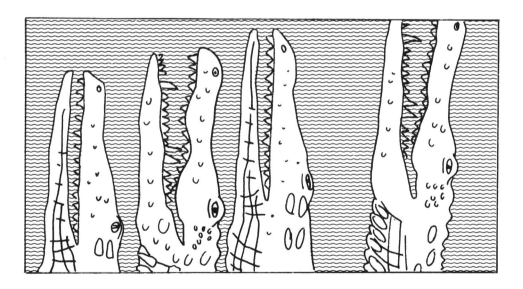

63. Which are the most dangerous crocodilians?

Any large crocodilian can and will attack a person on occasion. But the most notorious human eaters are the saltwater crocodile and the African or Nile crocodile. The American alligator does not usually attack people unless cornered or bothered in some way.

The saltwater crocodile of Asia and the Pacific is considered to be one of the most dangerous animals in the world. Over the years, they have killed and eaten many people. One of the most ghastly incidents involving these giant reptiles took place in the aftermath of World War II. In the winter of 1945, over one thousand Japanese soldiers were hemmed in by a British troop at the edge of a swamp on an island in the Bay of Bengal. The Japanese were knee deep in water and mud. The crocodiles moved in at nightfall. By the morning, only twenty men had survived the long night of crocodile attacks.

The African or Nile crocodile seems to attack people regularly in some areas but not in others. There is no doubt that this crocodile can be a real danger. The author of a recent book about the Nile crocodile recounts the death of a young Peace Corps volunteer on the banks of a river in Ethiopia. Some villages near rivers even build stockades to protect the places where people wash clothes and get drinking water. Other villages do not seem to have a problem with crocodiles.

64. Are poisonous lizards dangerous?

Only two kinds of lizards are poisonous, the Gila monster and the Mexican beaded lizard. They are found only in the southwestern

United States and Mexico. Both have a very powerful nerve poison that can cause injury and even death. But almost all of the reported cases of people being bitten occurred when the victim was handling the animal in a zoo, laboratory, or some display. Rarely do reports of attacks come from the wild. The poisonous lizards are dangerous to handle but easy to avoid in nature. These lizards would rather flee than fight.

65. Are turtles dangerous?

Turtles are reptiles (as are snakes, lizards, and crocodilians). Some people think that turtles are dangerous, but that's not really so. It is true that snapping turtles can bite a finger or a toe if it comes within reach, but that's true for almost any wild animal that's big enough. Some sea turtles have the reputation of being dangerous if they are bothered, but, again, that's true of almost any large animal. Even the largest sea turtles (some weigh nearly one thousand pounds) have not been known to attack people who don't bother them.

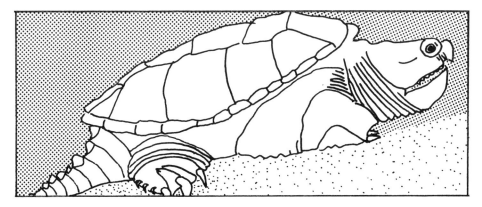

(10)

Sharks

66. How dangerous are sharks?

When the book and the movie *Jaws* appeared, some people became panicky. They were convinced that hungry sharks were just waiting for them in the ocean. Some moviegoers even decided to do their swimming in pools that summer. Others who saw the movie thought that *Jaws* was all nonsense. They said that no shark could rip a boat apart.

The truth about sharks lies somewhere in between. It is a fact that some kinds of sharks are dangerous and that there are many reported cases of shark attacks upon people. Some sharks have even been known to attack small boats and to sink them. But not every shark is a fearful giant that can rip a boat apart, let alone a person.

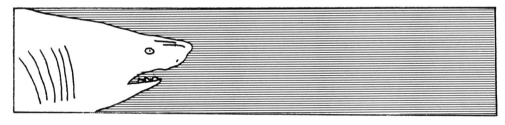

For example, the whale shark and the basking shark are
forty to fifty feet long; yet these giant sharks are quite harmless.
They feed on tiny sea animals by straining the water through their
mouths. Of course, these sharks are so large that they could
damage a boat if they thrashed about after someone hooked them.
But in that case, they would be no more dangerous than a large
whale.

There are about three hundred different kinds of sharks. Some
are only a foot or so long. Others are over fifty feet in length. Some
of these sharks are very dangerous; others are rarely involved in
attacks on people. Of course, unless you are an expert in dealing
with sharks, you would be best advised to get out of the water
promptly if a large shark cruises nearby.

67. How do sharks locate their prey?

Sharks do not have very large brains and may not be very bright,
but there is nothing wrong with their senses. They can zero in on a
meal from a great distance. Sharks have a row of nerve endings on
their bodies called a lateral line. The lateral line is sensitive to
sudden movements in the water. An animal or person thrashing
about in the water hundreds of feet away is enough to alert sharks
to the possibility of a meal.

Sharks also use their sense of smell and taste. In fact, a shark
can taste with sensory receptors on its head as well as with other
parts of its body. Sharks are very sensitive to the smell and taste of
blood. They can detect even a tiny amount of blood in many gallons
of seawater. Using feeling, smell, and taste, sharks home in on
their target.

68. Do sharks only attack under certain conditions?

There are many different theories about shark attacks. Here are some: Sharks attack only in warm waters. Sharks attack only in deep water. Sharks have to roll over on their backs to bite. Sharks attack only at night. Sharks attack only in the morning. Sharks do not attack in stormy weather. Sharks do not attack in bright sunlight.

The truth is that all of these theories about shark attacks are wrong. Sharks can attack in cold water or warm water, in deep water or shallow water, on their backs or right side up, at night or during the day, and in all kinds of weather. A dangerous shark is dangerous anywhere. Even when a shark is caught and brought aboard a boat, it can bite your hand or foot off.

69. Which sharks are the most dangerous?

About twenty to thirty different kinds of sharks are known to have attacked people. Of these dangerous sharks, the kinds most often mentioned are the great white, the mako, the hammerhead, the tiger, and the white-tipped.

70. How many shark attacks occur each year?

Experts say that about fifty unprovoked shark attacks occur each year around the world. Of course, this number does not take into account the many attacks that are never reported. People who rely on diving and fishing in the sea may very well become shark victims without the attacks being reported. Perhaps about one-third of the known shark attacks result in death.

71. How dangerous is the great white shark (*Jaws*)?

The great white shark is also called the human eater, a name that it well deserves. It is undoubtedly the most dangerous of the sharks. This huge and powerful killer of the seas may reach a length of fifty feet. It doesn't have to be that large to be dangerous, however. A twenty-foot great white can be quite a killer.

Not only does the great white attack people in the water, but it will also attack small boats. Few living things in the sea are safe when the shark is around. It eats seals, sea turtles, other sharks, and other large fish. It will even eat garbage dumped out by ships at sea.

The great white is found in all the tropical oceans of the world and sometimes in temperate seas. It has a huge set of jagged-edged teeth that can rip through flesh easily. A single tooth can be three inches long. Even its skin is dangerous. The shark's skin is like rough armor. You can cut your hand rubbing against the hundreds of thousands of tiny spines that cover the skin.

72. Is there any way to prevent a shark attack?

There is really no known way that you can prevent shark attacks absolutely. You are not going to stop a shark on the attack by hitting it on the nose or grabbing its fins or anything else. The best way is the most obvious: Get out of the water as soon as possible.

Here are a few rules that can minimize the danger of an attack: Stay out of the water if sharks are sighted or reported to be in the area. Do not swim with a bleeding wound. Always swim with a partner; you might be able to help each other if something goes wrong.

Sharks are very dangerous animals, but it doesn't make sense to worry about them all the time. Sharks kill far fewer people in ten years than are killed in automobile accidents in the United States over a single holiday weekend. And the number of automobile accidents doesn't necessarily stop you from going for a drive.

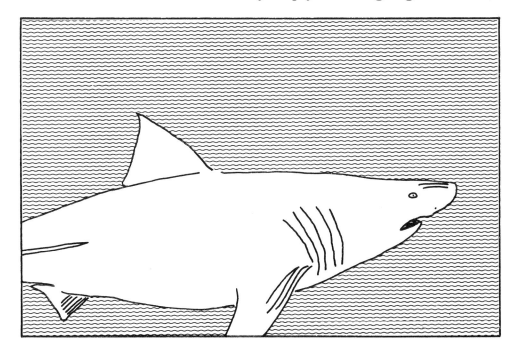

(11)

Dangerous Fish

73. What fish causes the most injuries?

Stingrays injure more people each year than does any other kind of fish, including sharks. In the United States alone, about one thousand people are injured each year by stingrays. Yet stingrays do not deliberately attack people. Every one of the injuries they cause is the result of an accident.

Stingrays are flat fish that hide at the bottom of the sea, partly hidden in sand or mud. The stingray has a long, whiplike tail. Along the top of the tail is a jagged spine, or stinger. When someone accidentally steps on one, the stingray swings its tail up and around and drives the stinger into the leg of the unfortunate person.

The wound can be five or six inches long and quite bad. Not only may the wound be deep, but the stingray also injects a poison that can cause severe pain and sickness. The spine sometimes also breaks off and remains in the wound. Many of the stingray's victims have to be hospitalized.

The several dozen different kinds of stingrays are found in all the warm oceans and in tropical rivers as well. Stingrays range in size. Some are as small as a pancake, while the Australian giant stingray can grow to fourteen feet in length and weigh more than seven hundred pounds.

74. Are devil rays dangerous?

Devil rays certainly look dangerous. They grow to weights of more than three thousand pounds and may reach twenty feet across from wing tip to wing tip. But their name and appearance give a wrong idea of their habits. Devil rays are not dangerous. They have never been known to harm a person deliberately, though a devil ray that's been harpooned may capsize a boat in an attempt to escape.

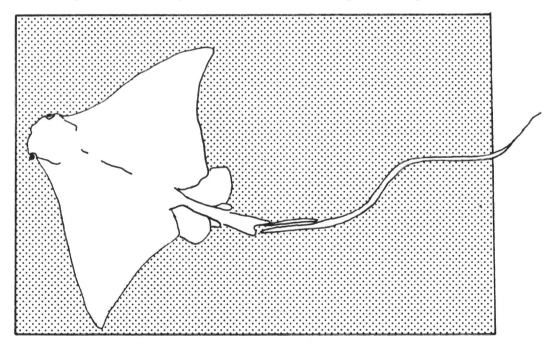

75. Is the barracuda dangerous?

There are a number of different kinds of fish called barracuda, and at least one of them is definitely dangerous. The great barracuda, sometimes called the "tiger of the sea," has been known to attack people. This giant can grow to a length of eight feet. Its mouth is huge and filled with razor-sharp, pointed teeth that could easily amputate a person's arm or leg in one bite. The shock and bleeding from an attack can cause death.

76. Is the moray eel dangerous?

Moray eels have powerful, muscular bodies that may reach six to ten feet in length. They have strong jaws armed with many sharp teeth that are good for tearing and holding on to their prey. Morays live in the cracks of rocks, in coral formations, or in old shipwrecks. They remain hidden from view until their prey comes close enough for them to strike.

Although the moray is sometimes hunted by scuba divers, most divers regard them as dangerous. Anyone sticking a hand or a foot into the hiding place of a moray eel is likely to be badly bitten. The bite is deep and often requires hospitalization. The moray is not poisonous, but the wound may become infected.

Moray eels do not hunt people. They will attack a person in self-defense if the person gets too close. Many people have been bitten by morays over the years, but there are no reports of any deaths being caused by these bites.

77. Are any other large fish dangerous?

Giant groupers or sea bass have been known to attack bathers or divers occasionally. Some of the larger groupers weigh up to five hundred pounds and have a hefty appetite. It is possible that some of these giants attack because they look on a person as a food animal. But generally there seems to be little danger to people from these fish.

There are many other large, powerful fish in the sea such as the swordfish, the marlin, and the sailfish. Some of these weigh more than one thousand pounds. When a fish that size with a hard beak hits a person, you can be sure that injuries will result. The danger to people comes from what happens when you try to hook and catch one of these giant fish. There are many reports of injuries to fishermen and of damage to their small boats. Yet these game fish are in far more danger from people than people are from them. Aside from those fish that are hunters, such as sharks and barracuda, fish usually will not attack people except in self-defense or by accident.

78. Is the piranha the most dangerous fish in the world?

In spite of its small size, the piranha has a giant reputation as a dangerous fish. The piranha is a freshwater fish native to South

America. It is only about a foot long, but it has powerful jaws with a row of razor-sharp teeth that fit into one another very closely.

The piranha can chop off a piece of meat or a finger or toe as quickly as a meat cleaver can. It has such powerful jaws that it can even bite through an ordinary fishhook or a piece of wood. The piranha swims in a school of hundreds. At the smell or taste of blood, the fish seem to go into a frenzy, snapping in all directions. A school of piranhas on the attack is like a thunderstorm of teeth and blood.

Wherever they are found, piranhas are feared by people. A school of piranhas has been known to strip the body of a large animal down to its bones in a matter of minutes. Their usual food is other fish and water animals; but mammals, birds, or any other animals that fall into the water become their game.

There are many reports and stories of people being killed by piranhas. Some of these tales are probably true, but others are undoubtedly fiction. It's hard to know which is which with some of the stories. It seems certain that the piranha is a dangerous fish and should be avoided. Whether it is the *most* dangerous fish in the world is open to question.

79. What is the most shocking fish in the world?

Without a doubt, the electric eel is the most "shocking" fish in the world. An electric eel can discharge more than one hundred

---

watts of electricity from thirty to three hundred times a second. That is enough to knock down a horse or knock out, or even kill, a person. There are several known cases of people being killed by electric eels.

An electric eel (not really an eel) can grow to a length of more than nine feet (mostly tail) and weigh up to ninety pounds. About two-thirds of the tail is made up of electric organs. The eel uses its electricity to stun or kill small fish and frogs and also to protect itself.

Electric eels live in some South American rivers and spend much of their time lying quietly in the water. Unlike most other fish, electric eels must come to the surface to gulp air. An electric eel will drown in ten minutes if it can't breathe air.

There are about thirty to forty electric fish in the world, but, except for the electric eel, most are fairly harmless to people. The only other exceptions are the torpedo rays, which live in warm ocean waters. These rays can give a fairly good shock to anyone who comes in contact with them.

80. What is the most poisonous fish in the world?

The stonefish and its close relatives are undoubtedly the most poisonous fish in the world. These fish have a series of spines on their backs. Each spine has a pair of small sacs of poison attached to it. Any pressure on the fish, such as someone stepping on it, will cause the sacs to eject the poison along grooves in the spine. The poison will enter the wound made by the sharp spine and cause terrible pain and even death.

The stonefish are found along the east coast of Africa, throughout the Indian Ocean, and in the waters around northern Australia and the South Pacific islands. A stonefish usually lies on the bottom around tropical coral reefs and rocks. It has a flattened, short body—less than a foot long—with a huge mouth. The fish is almost impossible to spot because it looks exactly like a piece of dead coral on the ground. The stonefish lies waiting until a small fish comes along, and then—snap—the fish is gone.

It is very difficult to protect yourself against accidentally stepping on a stonefish. They are not only impossible to spot, but their spines are also sharp enough to go through a pair of sneakers. Fortunately, there is an antivenin for the poison of the stonefish. Anyone who goes in areas where stonefish are found should be prepared to have to use it.

81. What is the most beautiful poisonous fish in the world?

While the poisonous stonefish is one of the ugliest of fish, the poisonous zebrafish is the most beautiful. This fish has become a fairly familiar sight in public and home aquariums. The zebrafish (it is also called the lionfish, the dragonfish, the turkeyfish, among other names) has beautiful dark stripes against a light background. It has large and showy fins. When it floats quietly in the water, the zebrafish looks like a creature from the imagination rather than like a real animal.

This beautiful fish is, however, quite poisonous. It has eighteen poisonous spines. The poison can be injected into a wound made by the spine. The amount of poison is much less than that of a stonefish. Even though the zebrafish is less dangerous than the stonefish, it can still cause great pain, that can last for a day or longer, and even death. Anyone who keeps the zebrafish in a home aquarium should never handle it without a net, even when the fish is dead.

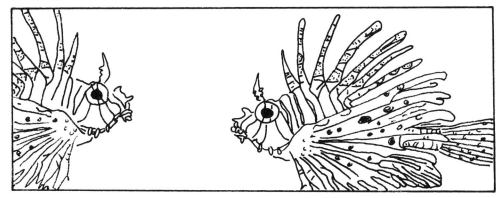

82. What are some other poisonous fish?

There is a group of poisonous fish commonly known as weevers that are dangerous if not handled properly. These fish are found in the North Sea, the Mediterranean, and the eastern Atlantic Ocean. They live in coastal waters and in shallow bays. They are probably the most poisonous fish found in the cooler waters of the Northern Hemisphere.

The weevers are only about one to one and a half feet long. They have a number of sharp spines along their backs as well as spines on either side of their heads. Each of the spines is poisonous and can cause terrible pain if it goes into a person's flesh. Weevers are fairly commonly used as a food fish and many tons are caught each year, so the chance of mishandling them is great.

A number of other poisonous fish have been reported to have caused injury and even death. Among these are a South American river-dwelling catfish with poisonous spines and many kinds of scorpion fish. The exact number of different kinds of poisonous fish is not known, but it may be about one hundred.

(12)

Insects, Spiders, and Scorpions

---

83. How dangerous are fire ants?

Fire ants don't look very different from the ordinary small brown ants that you may find in your house during the summer. But fire ants have stingers at the end of their bodies that they are quick to use on people or animals. The sting is poisonous, painful, and burns like fire.

Sometimes large numbers of fire ants will attack and sting a person dozens or even hundreds of times. The stings can cause severe illness or even death. Fire ants nesting around dwellings and in farmlands can be very dangerous to people. In some southern states there is a fire-ant mound every twenty-five feet. More than one hundred million acres in Texas and the southeastern United States are covered by mounds.

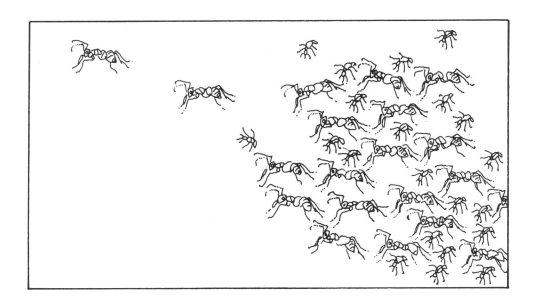

84. How large is a colony of army ants?

Army ants live in very large colonies. Even the smaller colonies have one hundred thousand ants in them. And the larger colonies contain over twenty million ants. That is more ants in one colony than there are people in the largest city in the world.

When an army ant colony is on the move, any animal caught in the middle is brought down and bitten to death by the thousands of attackers. There are many stories about people being caught and killed by army ants. But most of these tales are probably untrue. Almost anyone who can walk can move more quickly than an advancing column of army ants. Of course, an infant or an elderly or disabled person might not be able to flee fast enough and might be overrun and killed.

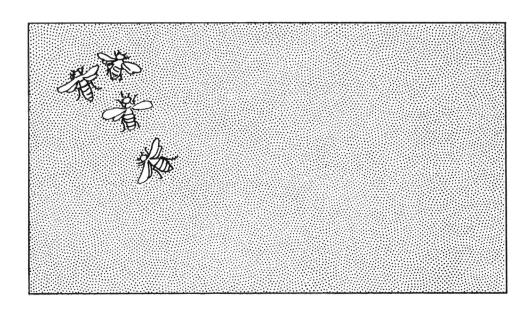

85. How dangerous are bee or wasp stings?

Bee or wasp stings can be very dangerous. At the least, a sting is very painful. A bee or wasp injects a number of different kinds of poison that affect the body in different ways. Some people may shrug off a sting as just an annoyance. But other people go into shock as their bodies react to the substances that the insect injected.

At one time, some people thought that a person would have to be stung many times to be in danger of dying. But nowadays, most scientists believe that the sting of even a single bee or wasp can cause death. In fact, bee or wasp stings probably cause more deaths in the United States than do poisonous snakebites.

A doctor once collected information on the number of people

who died in the United States from 1950 through 1954 as a result of poisonous bites and stings. He found that seventy-one people died from the bites of poisonous snakes, but eighty-six people died from the stings of wasps and bees.

86. Do bees and wasps die after stinging?

Many kinds of bees can sting only once. The stingers have barbs that catch on the skin and prevent the bee from pulling the stinger free. The bee is injured when it tries to pull away and dies in a short time. Wasps and hornets are different. Their stingers are not barbed. They may sting a person several times and not get their stingers caught.

87. How dangerous are flies and gnats?

Flies and gnats make their homes almost everywhere from the hot tropics to the cold climates and long winters of the far north and south. Some are very large; others, small; still others, almost too tiny to be seen. Some kinds help people by attacking other insects or by being scavengers. But other kinds bite people and carry disease.

The common housefly is not a biter, but it is a carrier of about thirty different kinds of diseases, including typhoid fever, plague, cholera, polio, and even leprosy. Flies are certainly not the only carriers of these diseases, but the housefly is widespread and comes in contact with many people around the world.

Many kinds of gnats are particularly dangerous. One kind of gnat in Europe attacks in swarms. The cloud of biting gnats is so thick that the gnat bites may even cause death because of the victim's loss of blood.

The tsetse fly of Africa is the carrier of the dreaded disease known as sleeping sickness. The disease causes permanent damage to a person's nervous system. Vast stretches of tropical Africa are unlivable because of the tsetse fly.

The screwworm fly is still another killer. The screwworm is found over the southern half of the United States, Mexico, and South and Central America. It bores into body tissues and lays its eggs inside a person or animal. The eggs hatch into tiny maggots called screwworms. The worms cause illness and death. Other similar flies cause the same kind of harm in tropical countries all over the world.

88. Are mosquitoes dangerous?

Not only do mosquitoes annoy people by their bites, but many kinds also carry dangerous diseases. Malaria, yellow fever, and other tropical diseases are carried by mosquitoes from one person to another. In some tropical countries, clouds of mosquitoes are so thick that people are blinded by so many bites. Even a single bite from a mosquito can be very harmful to a person who is allergic to it.

The mosquito's sound is made by the rapid movements of its wings. Some people think that a buzzing mosquito will not bite, but that is not true. What is true is that only the female mosquito bites. Male mosquitoes feed upon plant juices, never blood as do the females.

89. Are biting bugs dangerous?

Bedbugs and other bugs that bite and suck blood can be very dangerous. Some people go into shock and become very ill because they have an allergic reaction to the bug bite. Any bug bite has the potential of causing injury to a person who is allergic. Certain bugs are even poisonous. One such bug found in a few desert regions has been described by scientists as having a poison more deadly than that of a cobra.

90. Are dragonflies dangerous?

Despite such terrible nicknames as devil's darning needles, snake feeders, and mule stingers, dragonflies are not dangerous to people at all. In fact, they are really very helpful. Dragonflies do not sting people or large animals. They mostly eat flying insects such as flies and mosquitoes and help keep down the numbers of those harmful insects.

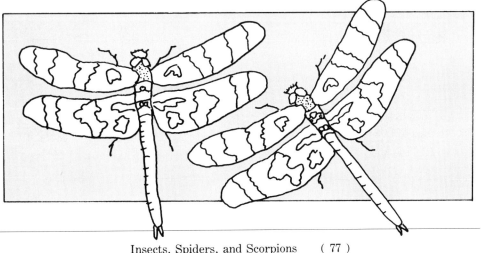

Insects, Spiders, and Scorpions (77)

91. How dangerous is the black widow spider?

The black widow is the most poisonous spider in the United States. The bite of the female black widow (the male doesn't bite) usually is not deadly, but it can be very painful. There is now an antivenin for the black widow poison, so death from the bite is very rare.

The black widow is a small, shiny black spider with a red hourglass-shaped mark on its underside. The female is usually less than a half-inch long. The spiders are common in many areas of the United States and Mexico. They are also found throughout South and Central America. They live in cool, dark spots and are very shy, so they are rarely seen.

The black widow spider is so named because the female eats the male after mating. The young spiders also eat one another. This kind of behavior is shared by other spiders as well. But as far as people are concerned, the black widow's reputation is worse than her bite.

92. How dangerous are tarantulas?

The name tarantula strikes fear into many people. The word is a common name for any large, hairy spider in any part of the world. The American tarantula is about two inches long and has a leg spread of four to five inches. Some may think that the American tarantula is not very pretty, but it is one of the most harmless of all spiders. It will bite only in self-defense if handled roughly, and its bite is only mildly poisonous. The wound may be a bit painful, but not more so than a bee sting.

93. Are all spiders dangerous?

To many people, all spiders are horrible. They think that all spiders are ready to bite the first person who comes near. These people couldn't be more wrong. Spiders are far more useful than harmful to people. Most spiders are insect eaters. They are not destructive, do not usually carry diseases, and do not eat our food. Only the few spiders that are poisonous are dangerous to any degree.

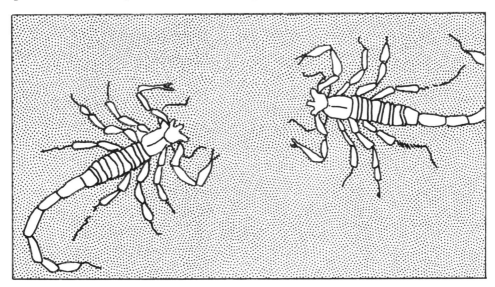

94. Are scorpions dangerous?

In the United States and Mexico, many more people are killed by scorpions than by poisonous snakes. There are many different kinds of scorpions found in warm, dry areas around the world. All have a tail section that is armed with a curved stinger at the tip. The stinger is attached to poison glands. A scorpion will defend itself by arching the stinger over its back and waving it in all directions.

In the larger kinds of scorpions, the stinger is big and the amount of poison plentiful. Scorpions are very common in and around houses and are frequently found hiding in bedclothes, shoes, and other articles that humans use. For this reason, there are many cases of people being stung by scorpions.

95. Are millipedes and centipedes dangerous?

Millipedes usually feed upon decaying plant materials. They do not bite and are usually safe to handle. Centipedes do bite and can give a person a painful wound. The larger centipedes in the United States can grow to over six inches in length and are mildly poisonous, so they should be avoided. Still larger centipedes in tropical countries grow to one foot in length and their bite can be very severe.

(13)

Dangerous Sea Animals

96. Is the octopus dangerous?

There are about fifty different kinds of octopuses. They range in size from one inch to over twenty-five feet long, but only a few kinds are over two feet. An octopus is generally very shy and will usually hide or flee rather than confront a person. But if an octopus is attacked and cornered, it may try to hold on with its tentacles. If the octopus is a large one, its grip may be strong enough to hold a person below the surface long enough to drown. But this has rarely occurred, and the octopus is not really a dangerous animal. Most of the stories you read about octopus attacks on people only happened in the writer's imagination.

97. Is the giant squid dangerous?

The giant squid, called the kraken after the legendary monster, is the largest animal without a backbone in the world. No one knows for sure just how large kraken may become, but some are over fifty feet long and weigh more than a ton. They live in the open sea, and few live ones have ever been seen. Sometimes, dead kraken are cast ashore on beaches, and those are the ones that are measured.

The original kraken was a creature of legends. Some were said to have wrapped their huge tentacles around sailing ships and dragged the ships below the waves. Others were said to have reached aboard ships and snatched sailors from the decks.

It is said by some fishermen that a kraken's beak can bite more deeply than can that of a shark. It is true that captured sperm whales often are heavily scarred by the sucker marks of the kraken's tentacles.

Are any of the other stories true? Is the kraken dangerous to people? As for the giant kraken attacking ships, it is impossible to say. The stories are very old, the witnesses are dead, and there are no photographs. You can pretty much believe what you like. As to the chances of meeting a kraken in the water, it is very unlikely unless you like swimming in deep ocean waters at night. If you were to meet a large kraken at sea, it probably would be a good idea to get out of the water promptly. Realistically, you have little to worry about from the kraken.

98. Can a giant clam hold a person under the water?

The giant clam is often more than three or four feet long and can weigh over five hundred pounds. The outer edge of each shell is deeply waved and can fit closely into the opposite shell. The giant clam is found in the waters of the South Pacific, the East Indies, and the east coast of Africa. One of these giant clams can provide a lot of clam chowder to the people who dive for them.

Are any of these divers ever caught and held underwater by

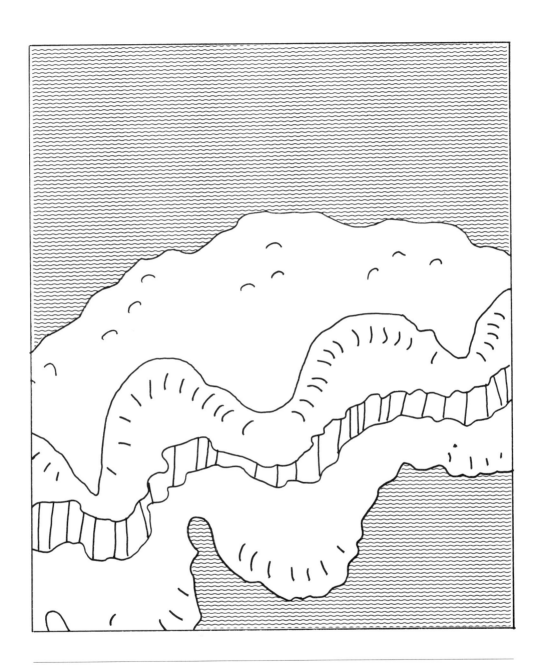

Dangerous Sea Animals　　(83)

this giant? There are certainly many tales of people getting an arm or leg caught in a closing clam and being held underwater until they were drowned. But most of these tales are probably untrue. The giant clam closes so slowly that it is unlikely to grab a person's arm or leg before it could be snatched away. Some scientists think that there have been a few cases where people have been hurt; other scientists think not. No one seems to know for sure.

99. Are jellyfish dangerous?

Free-floating jellyfish don't look very threatening, but their stings can be harmful and even deadly. Jellyfish usually have many tentacles hanging from a rounded, jellylike middle. The tentacles contain poisonous stingers that are released when trigger tentacles are touched. The stingers can cause severe pain, rashes, illness, and even death.

Some of the most dangerous jellyfish are found in the waters off Australia and throughout the southwest Pacific and Indian oceans. The most dangerous jellyfish are the different kinds of sea wasps and box jellies. One of the most deadly sea wasps is common from the Philippines to Australia. It is said to have caused many deaths. The poison is so deadly that the victim experiences pain immediately and may die within a few minutes. Anyone stung by this jellyfish in deep water would probably drown and be lost without a trace.

100. How dangerous is the Portuguese man-of-war?

The Portuguese man-of-war is not really a jellyfish, but it is closely related. The six-inch balloon is the only part that you see above the surface. But underneath the balloon are tentacles hanging down, sometimes thirty to forty feet. Along the tentacles are stinging cells that can hurt you as badly as the sting of a bee or wasp. Stings from a man-of-war are sometimes bad enough to require hospitalization, but they rarely result in death.

Swimmers coming in contact with the tentacles can be in terrible agony. Each tentacle can leave a mark like the lash of a whip. The scars can last a lifetime. The tentacles can still sting even when the man-of-war is beached on the sand, dead and apparently harmless.

(14)

The Most Dangerous Animal in the World

101. What is the most dangerous animal in the world?

In The Bronx Zoo there is a sign that reads: THE MOST DANGEROUS ANIMAL IN THE WORLD. Underneath the sign is a window. When people look into the window, they find that it is a mirror. Then they know the truth.

The most dangerous animal in the world to people is people themselves. The number of people killed or injured by other people in wars, riots, battles, fights, and crimes far exceeds the number wounded by any wild animal. As the cartoon character Pogo once said, "We have met the enemy, and he is us."

Index

flies, 75–76
foxes, 18

gnats, 75–76
gorillas, 19, 20
great white sharks, 24, 60, 61

hawks, 38
hippopotamuses, 28
hyenas, 17–18

insects, 47, 72–80

jackals, 18
jaguars, 1, 2, 7
jellyfish, 84

leopards, 1, 2, 5, 6
lions, 1, 2, 4–5, 30
lizards, 56–57

mambas, 46, 51
millipedes, 80
monkeys, 22
mosquitoes, 76

octopuses, 81
orang-utans, 20
ostriches, 39–40

panthers, black, 5
people, 86
pigs, wild, 29
piranhas, 66–67
Portuguese men-of-war, 84–85
pumas, American, 1, 2, 5, 7–9

pythons, 42, 43–44

rats, 33–34
rattlesnakes, 46, 48–49
rays, 63-64, 68
reptiles, 42–57
rhinoceroses, 27–28
rodents, 33-34, 48

scarlet king snakes, 46–47
scorpions, 79–80
seals, leopard, 25–26
sea snakes, 50-51
sharks, 24, 58–62
shrews, 32
snakes, 42–53
spiders, 78–79
squids, giant (krakens), 81–82
stingrays, 63-64
stonefish, 68–69, 70

tarantulas, 78
tigers, 1–4
turtles, 57

vipers, 51–52
vultures, 38

walruses, 26
wasps, 74–75
weasels, 18
whales, 23–25
wolverines, 18
wolves, 14–15

zebrafish, 70